Just Say the Word!

Do you know that
ONE word can have
TWO different meanings ?
See if you know that word
for each page, and then
check the numbers at the back
to see if you got them !

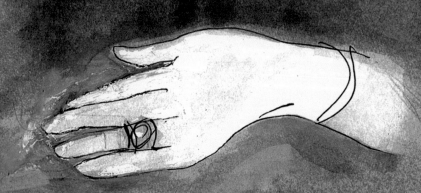

FOREVER/USA

NOW LET'S SEE
IF YOU SAID
THE WORD...

DID YOU SAY THESE WORDS?

1. trunk
2. tie
3. glasses
4. waves
5. chest
6. horn
7. pitcher
8. ruler
9. bark
10. flies
11. cold
12. train
13. trip
14. ring
15. stamp
16. file
17. nails
18. watch
19. bat   *Can you think of any more words?*

To order additional copies of this book, contact:
Xlibris
844-714-8691
www.Xlibris.com
Orders@Xlibris.com

ISBN: 978-1-5434-9877-6 (sc)
ISBN: 978-1-5434-9878-3 (hc)
ISBN: 978-1-5434-9876-9 (e)

Library of Congress Control Number: 2021919918

Print information available on the last page

Rev. date: 10/13/2021

Printed in the United States
by Baker & Taylor Publisher Services